SATURDAY SANCOCHO

Leyla Torres

SQUARE FISH

FARRAR STRAUS GIROUX / NEW YORK

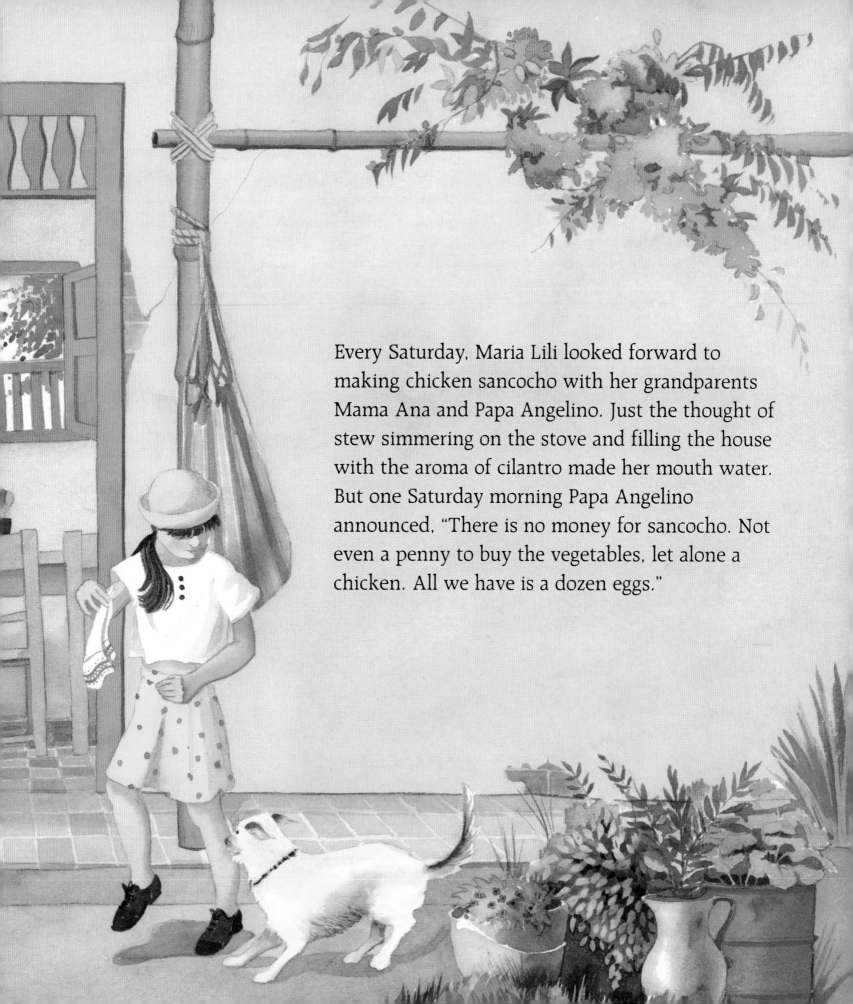

Every Saturday, Maria Lili looked forward to making chicken sancocho with her grandparents Mama Ana and Papa Angelino. Just the thought of stew simmering on the stove and filling the house with the aroma of cilantro made her mouth water. But one Saturday morning Papa Angelino announced, "There is no money for sancocho. Not even a penny to buy the vegetables, let alone a chicken. All we have is a dozen eggs."

"Then we will use the eggs to make sancocho," replied Mama Ana.

"Egg sancocho! Everyone knows sancocho is not prepared with eggs," said Maria Lili.

Smiling, Mama Ana removed her apron and asked Maria Lili to take two baskets and place the eggs in one of them.

"Come, my dear, we are going to the market."

And off they went.

At the market square they walked from stall to stall. First they found Don Eugenio and his son, Sebastian. Mama Ana persuaded Don Eugenio to accept six eggs for a bunch of green plantains. It did not take much bargaining, Sebastian was one of Maria Lili's classmates.

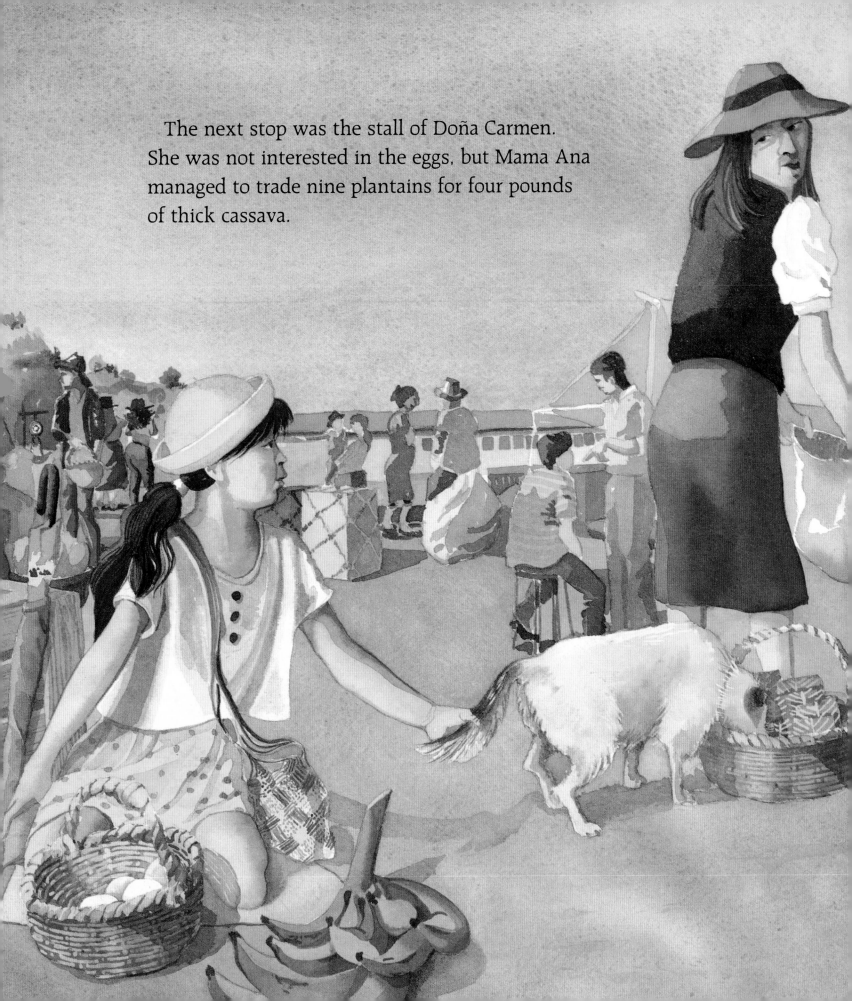

The next stop was the stall of Doña Carmen.
She was not interested in the eggs, but Mama Ana
managed to trade nine plantains for four pounds
of thick cassava.

At first Don Mateo was not in the mood for
bartering. It took some time for Mama Ana to
convince him to take two pounds of cassava for
six ears of corn. She gave him a couple of eggs as
well. "So he doesn't pout," Mama Ana whispered,
making sure the corn was fresh.

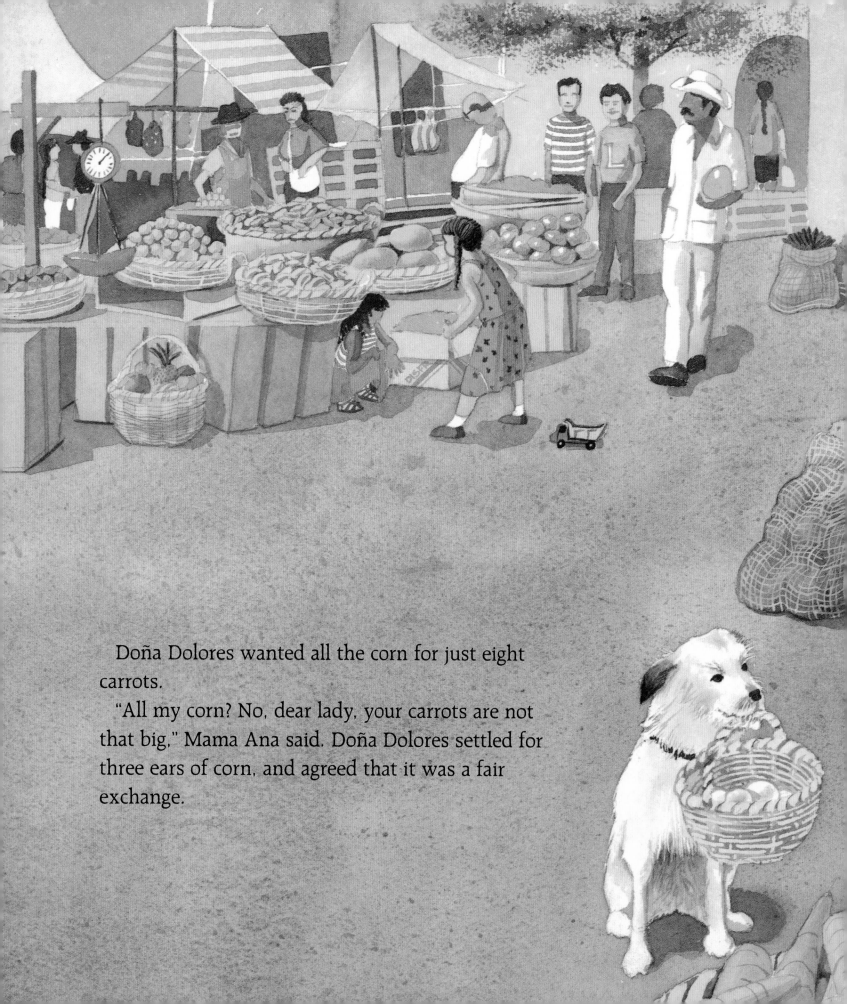

Doña Dolores wanted all the corn for just eight carrots.

"All my corn? No, dear lady, your carrots are not that big," Mama Ana said. Doña Dolores settled for three ears of corn, and agreed that it was a fair exchange.

Under the noonday sun, Mama Ana and Maria Lili traded their remaining eggs for onions and tomatoes; tomatoes for cilantro; cilantro for garlic and garlic for cumin, always keeping some for themselves. But they still needed one more ingredient.

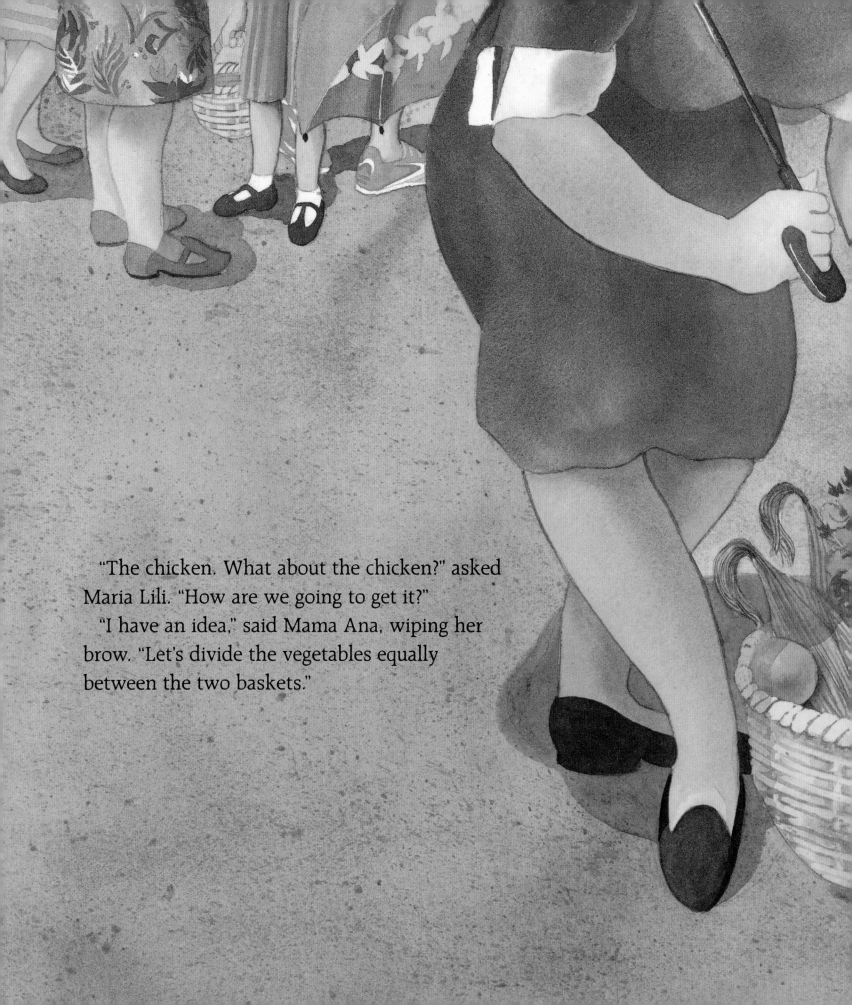

"The chicken. What about the chicken?" asked Maria Lili. "How are we going to get it?"

"I have an idea," said Mama Ana, wiping her brow. "Let's divide the vegetables equally between the two baskets."

Mama Ana offered one of the baskets to Doña Petrona in exchange for a large, red-feathered chicken.

"Impossible," Doña Petrona said, sniffing. "I'll give you this one instead." She showed Mama Ana a smaller one.

"No, it's much too skinny," said Mama Ana, frowning.

They haggled until Mama Ana added two more carrots and some cumin to the basket. Doña Petrona accepted the offer, handing Maria Lili a nice, potbellied chicken. It was not the largest one, but it was good enough for a wholesome stew.

As Mama Ana and Maria Lili were leaving the marketplace, they passed Don Fernando's stall. He had always admired Mama Ana's hand-knit bags and suggested they trade the one Maria Lili was carrying for one of his wooden ladles. With a wink, he also handed her a colorful spinning top.

Papa Angelino plucked the chicken while Mama
Ana boiled the water and peeled the vegetables.
Maria Lili chopped the onions and the cilantro.
This was a teary job.

That afternoon, no later than usual, they sat down to enjoy their chicken sancocho. Maria Lili ate slowly, blowing gently on each spoonful. The stew was delicious.

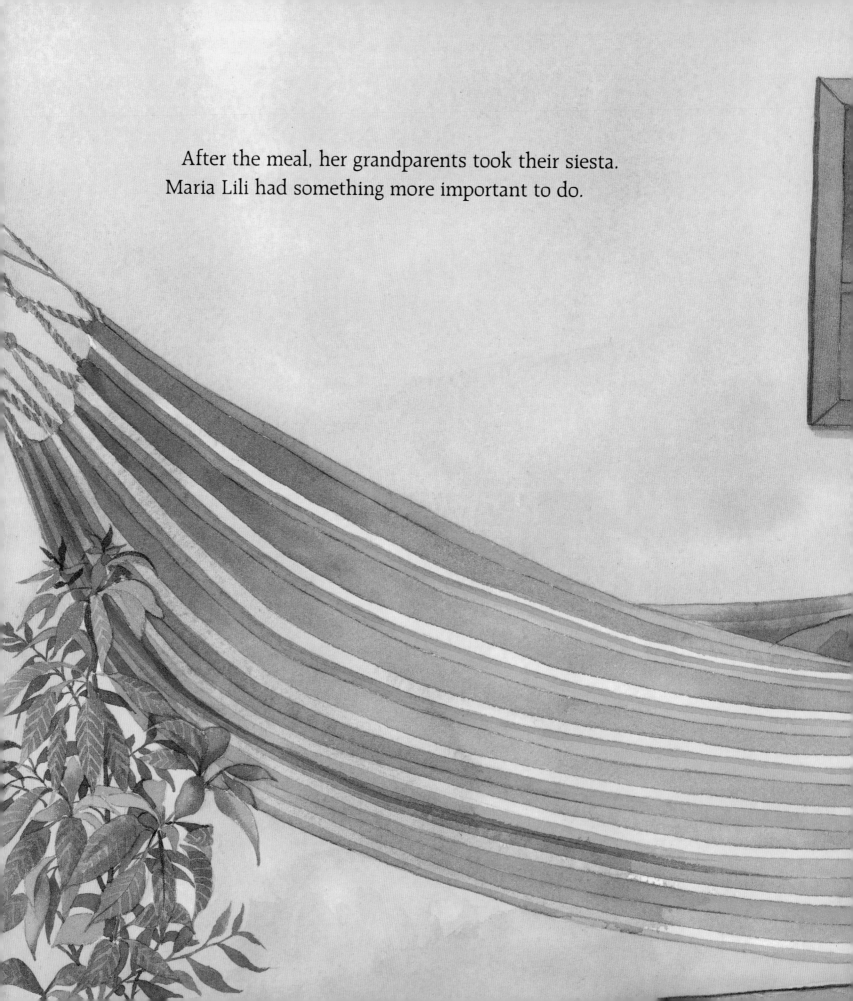

After the meal, her grandparents took their siesta.
Maria Lili had something more important to do.

The main ingredients in sancocho are chicken, beef, or fish, and an assortment of vegetables such as corn, carrots, squash, and potatoes. Though this stew is prepared differently throughout Central and South America, cassava (or *yuca*) and green plantains are always key ingredients. The following recipe, like so many great family secrets, has been handed down from one generation to the next.

Mama Ana's Chicken Sancocho

2 medium onions, chopped

2 cloves garlic, minced

1 1/2 teaspoons salt

1 (3-pound) broiler-fryer chicken, cut into pieces

2 green plantains, peeled and cut into thirds

2 ears corn, husked and cut into fourths

1 large cassava, peeled and cut into large pieces

3 carrots, quartered

1 bunch fresh cilantro, chopped

2 tablespoons vegetable oil

4 small tomatoes, chopped

1 teaspoon cumin

salt and pepper to taste

additional chopped cilantro for garnish

In a 6-quart soup pot combine 2 quarts water, half the onion and garlic, and salt; bring to a boil. Add chicken. Cover and reduce heat; simmer 10 minutes. Add plantains and corn; simmer 5 more minutes. Add cassava, carrots, and cilantro. Let simmer 40 minutes, or until vegetables are tender.

In a skillet, heat oil; add the rest of the garlic and onion. Cook until soft, stirring occasionally. Add tomatoes and cook 2 to 3 minutes. Stir in cumin, salt, and pepper.

Transfer stew to a large serving bowl and spoon tomato mixture over chicken; top with additional chopped cilantro. Serves four.

Remember to have an adult help you in the kitchen.

For my parents, Luis Eduardo and Rosalba

SQUARE FISH

An imprint of Macmillan Publishing Group, LLC
120 Broadway, New York, NY 10271 • mackids.com
Copyright © 1995 by Leyla Torres.
All rights reserved.
Square Fish and the Square Fish logo are trademarks of Macmillan and are used by Farrar Straus Giroux under license from Macmillan.
Our books may be purchased in bulk for promotional, educational, or business use.
Please contact your local bookseller or the Macmillan Corporate and Premium Sales Department at (800) 221-7945 ext. 5442
or by email at MacmillanSpecialMarkets@macmillan.com.

The Library of Congress has cataloged the hardcover edition as follows:
Library of Congress Cataloging-in-Publication Data
Torres, Leyla.
Saturday sancocho / Leyla Torres.
p. cm.
[1. Cookery – Fiction. 2. Barter – Fiction. 3. Grandmothers – Fiction. 4. South America – Fiction.] I. Title.
P27.T6457Sat 1995 [E]-dc20 94-31329 CIP AC

Originally published in the United States by Farrar Straus Giroux
First Square Fish edition, 2022
Square Fish logo designed by Filomena Tuosto
Printed in China by RR Donnelley Asia Printing Solutions Ltd., Dongguan City, Guangdong Province.

ISBN 978-1-250-82555-1 (paperback)
1 3 5 7 9 10 8 6 4 2

AR: 4.4 / LEXILE: AD870L